I Can Draw!
¡Sé dibujar!

by Deborah Schecter

ISBN: 978-1-338-70293-4
Illustrated by Anne Kennedy
Copyright © 2020 by Deborah Schecter. All rights reserved.
Published by Scholastic Inc., 557 Broadway, New York, NY 10012

10 9 8 7 6   68   23 24 25 26/0

Printed in Jiaxing, China. First printing, June 2020.

■SCHOLASTIC

I can draw a seal.

Sé dibujar una foca.

I can draw a clown.

Sé dibujar un payaso.

I can draw a king.

Sé dibujar un rey.

I can draw a crown.

Sé dibujar una corona.

I can draw a sheep.

Sé dibujar una oveja.

I can draw a bed.

Sé dibujar una cama.

I can draw myself to sleep.

Puedo dibujar
hasta quedarme dormida.